Leonardo
the
TERRIBLE
MONSTER

FOR **THE TRIXTER,**
MY OWN LITTLE MONSTER

No part of this publication may be reproduced, stored in a retrieval system, or transmitted in any
form or by any means, electronic, mechanical, photocopying, recording, or otherwise, without
written permission of the publisher. For information regarding permission, write to
Hyperion Books for Children, an imprint of Disney Book Group,
125 West End Avenue, New York, NY 10023.

ISBN 978-1-338-34363-2

The publisher does not have any control over and does not assume any responsibility for author
or third-party websites or their content.

12 11 10 9 8 7 6 5 4 3 2   18 19 20 21 22 23

Printed in the U.S.A.   169

First Scholastic printing, September 2018

YOUR PAL MO WILLEMS PRESENTS

Leonardo

the

TERRIBLE

MONSTER

SCHOLASTIC INC.

LEONARDO

WAS A

TERRIBLE

MONSTER...

HE COULDN'T SCARE ANYONE.

HE DIDN'T HAVE 1,642* TEETH, LIKE TONY.

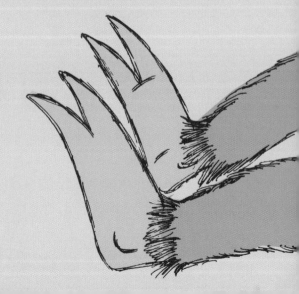

*NOTE: NOT ALL TEETH SHOWN.

HE
WASN'T
BIG,
LIKE
ELEANOR.

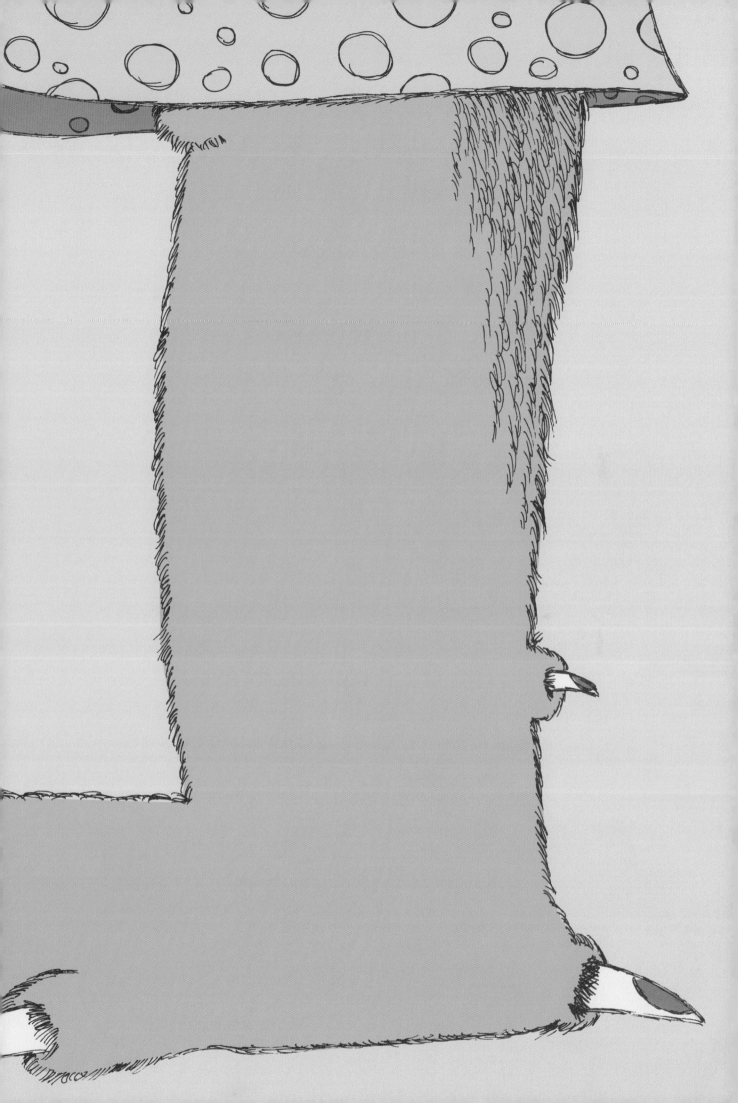

AND HE WASN'T JUST PLAIN WEIRD, LIKE HECTOR.

LEONARDO TRIED VERY HARD TO BE SCARY.

BUT...

HE JUST WASN'T.

ONE DAY,
LEONARDO HAD AN IDEA.
HE WOULD FIND THE MOST
SCAREDY-CAT KID IN
THE WHOLE WORLD...

AND SCARE THE
TUNA SALAD
OUT OF HIM!

LEONARDO RESEARCHED

UNTIL HE FOUND THE PERFECT CANDIDATE...

SAM.

LEONARDO SNUCK UP ON THE POOR, UNSUSPECTING BOY.

AND THE

MONSTER GAVE IT

ALL HE HAD.

UNTIL
THE LITTLE BOY
CRIED.

"YES!" CHEERED LEONARDO. "I DID IT! I'VE FINALLY SCARED THE TUNA SALAD OUT OF SOMEONE!"

"NO YOU DIDN'T!"
SNAPPED SAM.

"OH, YEAH?"
REPLIED
LEONARDO.
"THEN WHY
ARE YOU
CRYING?"

"MY MEAN BIG BROTHER STOLE
OF MY HANDS WHILE I WAS STILL
BROKE IT ON PURPOSE, AND IT
TRIED TO FIX IT BUT I COULDN'T,
TABLE AND I STUBBED MY TOE
LAST MONTH WHEN I ACCIDENTALLY
I GOT SOAP IN MY EYES TRYING TO
THAT MY BROTHER'S COCKATOO
DON'T HAVE ANY FRIENDS AND

MY ACTION FIGURE RIGHT OUT PLAYING WITH IT, AND THEN HE WAS MY FAVORITE TOY, AND I AND I GOT SO MAD I KICKED THE ON THE SAME FOOT THAT I HURT SLIPPED IN THE BATHTUB AFTER WASH OUT THE BIRD POO POOPED ON MY HEAD AND I MY TUMMY HURTS!"

THAT'S WHY.

THEN
LEONARDO
MADE

A
VERY
BIG
DECISION.

INSTEAD OF BEING
A TERRIBLE MONSTER,
HE WOULD BECOME
A WONDERFUL FRIEND.

(BUT THAT DIDN'T MEAN
THAT HE COULDN'T TRY
TO SCARE HIS FRIEND
EVERY NOW AND THEN!)

BOO!